CREATURE CAMPERS
THE WALL OF DOOM

WARNING!
ENTER AT OWN RISK!
THIS MEANS YOU!
OBSTACLE COURSE AHEAD!

JOE McGEE
ILLUSTRATED BY BEA TORMO

Andrews McMeel
PUBLISHING®

THE WALL OF DOOM

Andrews McMeel Publishing
a division of Andrews McMeel Universal
1130 Walnut Street, Kansas City, Missouri 64106

www.andrewsmcmeel.com

Epic! Creations, Inc.
702 Marshall Street, Suite 280, Redwood City, California 94063

www.getepic.com

20 21 22 23 24 SDB 10 9 8 7 6 5 4 3 2 1

Paperback ISBN: 978-1-5248-6090-5
Hardback ISBN: 978-1-5248-6143-8

Library of Congress Control Number: 2020930353

Design by Ariana Abud and Wendy Gable

Made by:
King Yip (Dongguan) Printing & Packaging Factory Ltd.
Address and location of production:
Daning Administrative District, Humen Town
Dongguan Guangdong, China 523930
1st Printing—6/6/20

ATTENTION: SCHOOLS AND BUSINESSES
Andrews McMeel books are available at quantity discounts with
bulk purchase for educational, business, or sales promotional use.
For information, please e-mail the Andrews McMeel Publishing
Special Sales Department: specialsales@amuniversal.com

Norm had to admit that Pa had been right: Camp Moonlight was certainly a lot of fun. As Norm got ready for the morning's activities, he thought about his time there so far. He'd learned how to canoe (and had met a real live lake creature!), found his way through the woods with a map and compass (even when the sky seemed to be falling), made some really great friends, *and* had almost all the berry casserole he could eat.

Almost.

Norm could eat berry casserole until there was no more berry casserole left to eat.

"Good morning, Creature Campers," said Furrow Grumplestick, the camp director. The bushy-bearded gnome stood before Cabin 4 with his clipboard in hand and a whistle around his neck.

Zeena Morf, their camp counselor, stood next to him. She was also wearing a whistle. And sneakers. And a sweatband. She looked like she was ready to go running.

Norm hoped they weren't going running. He did not like running. He was more of a strider.

"What's with the whistles?" asked Oliver. He didn't like running either. He was more of a walker.

"And the sweatband?" asked Wisp. Wisp was more of a flyer . . . of short distances.

Hazel bounded into the cabin. "Are we going running?" she asked. "I hope we're going running. Ooh, please tell me we're going running. I really hope we're going running. I looooooovvvvvve running!"

Hazel was absolutely a runner.

"*We* are not going running," began Grumplestick.

"Oh drat," said Hazel.

Norm, Oliver, and Wisp smiled.

"You are," finished Grumplestick.

The smiles disappeared.

"Yay!" said Hazel.

"Today is the obstacle course challenge," said Zeena.

"Obstacle course?" Norm asked.

"Challenge?" Oliver asked.

"That's right," said Grumplestick. "The famous Camp Moonlight obstacle course." He pulled a rolled-up length of paper from under his hat and handed it to Zeena.

Zeena unrolled it and held it up for Norm, Oliver, Wisp, and Hazel to see. It was a map of the obstacle course. Grumplestick pulled a wooden pointer from his beard and smacked the first obstacle.

"Your first challenge is the monkey bars . . . of doom!"

"Doom?" Norm asked.

"There's no doom," Zeena said. "Just mud. Lots and lots of ooey, gooey mud."

"Mud . . . ," said Grumplestick, "of doom!"

"No doom," said Zeena.

"From there, you'll move to," Grumplestick smacked the next part of the map, "the tires . . . of doom!"

"What's so dangerous about them?" asked Norm.

"Yeah, what's the doom?" asked Oliver.

"There is no doom," said Zeena.

Grumplestick frowned at Zeena. "Why do you have to ruin all of the fun?" he asked.

Zeena rolled her eyes.

"What's the third obstacle?" asked Hazel.

"And why is there a skull and crossbones on the map at the third obstacle?" Wisp added.

Grumplestick grinned.

"That," he said, "is the wall . . . "

"Of doom," said Norm, Oliver, Wisp, and Hazel.

"No doom," Zeena sighed.

MEANWHILE...

From inside a fake boulder not too far from where the Creature Campers listened to Furrow Grumplestick explain the obstacle course (of doom!), a familiar carnival owner heard every word.

"An obstacle course, eh?" said Barnaby Snoop. "One good turn deserves another, that's what I always say. Barnaby, old chap,

this may very well be your opportunity to return the favor those Creature Campers did for you when they saved you from that out-of-control supermagnet. I'll simply give them a little help when they need it, and we'll be even. It can't get any easier."

Barnaby Snoop rubbed his hands together and chuckled.

"Barnaby Snoop," he said, "you are one clever fellow. One clever fellow, indeed! And really, quite a decent gentleman all around."

Norm, Oliver, Wisp, and Hazel followed Grumplestick and Zeena to the Camp Moonlight activity field.

"Okay, Creature Campers," Zeena said. "We're going to begin with some light stretching."

"Of DOOM!" said Grumplestick.

Everyone stared at the gnome.

"Kidding!" Grumplestick said. "I'm kidding."

Norm cracked his knuckles and stretched his long arms out in front of himself. "We'll be through that obstacle course in no time."

"Piece of cake," said Wisp.

"We could do it blindfolded!" Hazel shouted.

"Oh really?" said Grumplestick. "You're on."

Norm was suddenly not so confident. "Blindfolded?" he asked.

"But how are we supposed to even see what we're doing?" asked Oliver.

"You'll have to depend on each other," said Grumplestick. "Only *one* of you will be allowed to see at each obstacle, and that camper will have to guide the rest of you." Grumplestick smiled. "Easy, right? Piece of cake. No sweat."

The Creature Campers, however, were now sweating. This was *not* going to be as easy as they'd thought.

"I see you're already working up a light sweat," said Zeena. "Good. Now let's start with some small arm circles, like this."

Zeena stretched her arms out to her sides and moved them in small circles. After the arm circles came toe touches, jumping jacks, and jogging in place.

"You're now ready to tackle the Camp Moonlight obstacle course," Zeena declared.

"If you successfully complete the obstacle course in time—"

"Wait, this is timed?" Oliver asked.

"It is," Zeena said. She held up a stopwatch.

"We're doomed!" said Wisp.

"See?" said Grumplestick, grinning. "I told you: doom."

"Ahem," said Zeena. "As I was saying, if you successfully complete the obstacle course in time, you will have your names added to the wall."

"How many names are on the wall?" asked Norm.

"One," said Grumplestick. He grinned through his beard and jabbed a thumb at his chest. "Mine."

Furrow Grumplestick and Zeena Morf led
Norm, Oliver, Hazel, and Wisp to the start
of the obstacle course.

As they stood next to a set of monkey
bars that stretched over a giant pit of mud,
they saw an old wooden sign pounded into
the ground. It read:

"A bit much, isn't it?" Norm asked.

"Is it?" asked Grumplestick. He pointed past the sign. "There's where the obstacle course ends."

The campers looked where Grumplestick pointed. Then they looked up. They looked up higher. They looked up until they could not look up any higher. They craned their necks and looked up toward the clouds at a wooden wall that loomed over the forest.

"How have we not seen that before?" Oliver asked.

"Because there's an invisibility field around it," said Zeena. "Alien technology."

She produced a controller from behind her back and pressed a button. The wall disappeared. She pressed it again, and it reappeared.

"Cool!" Wisp said.

"Do it again! Do it again!" said Hazel.

"I'd rather not," said Zeena. "I don't want to waste the—"

Hazel snatched the controller from Zeena's hand and pressed the button over and over and over.

"On. Off. On. Off. On. Off. On. Off. On. Off. On. Off. On . . . hey, why won't it go back off?"

"—batteries," Zeena finished, snatching the controller back from Hazel.

"Great," said Norm. "Now we can't even see the wall."

Hazel turned red. "Sorry," she said.

"Okay, enough fooling around," said Grumplestick. "You have twenty minutes to get through the obstacle course. Zeena will keep time. Any questions? None? Good. Let's get started." He reached under his hat and produced four strips of cloth. "Your blindfolds."

Norm had a very bad feeling about this.

MEANWHILE...

"Blindfolds?" said Barnaby Snoop. "That hardly seems fair. Perhaps they'll need more of my help than I thought."

He climbed into his hot air balloon and pulled up the anchor. He floated until he was hidden in a small patch of clouds just above the obstacle course.

"By the time anyone suspects they

might have had help, I'll be up, up, and away. Helping those Creature Campers get their names on the wall is the least I can do for them."

A bird landed on top of his balloon.

It looked at Barnaby. It looked at the balloon. It pecked the balloon once. Twice.

"Shoo!" said Barnaby. "Get off of there! Go! Shoo!"

The bird pecked away madly and then took off, flapping away over the forest and over the invisible wall.

Barnaby Snoop shook his fist at the bird. "Nothing will foil my plans this time. Not a meddlesome bird. Not a lake creature. Not a magnetic meteor. Not even that grumpy little gnome. Nothing!"

Barnaby's balloon began to descend.

A giant hiss of air escaped from where the bird had pecked.

"No!" said Barnaby. "No, no, no!"

Barnaby Snoop grabbed a small patch, a needle, and some thread and scrambled up to repair his balloon. He had a leak to fix. And a Bigfoot to help. And nothing, *nothing,* was going to stop him.

Well, almost nothing. If that leak wasn't fixed soon, that might stop him.

I'M CERTAINLY AWARE OF THAT!

Norm, Hazel, Oliver, and Wisp stared at the monkey bars, which stretched across a pit of thick, ooey, gooey, squishy mud. If the campers slipped and fell off . . . SPLAT! Into the mud they would go. If they missed a bar and fell . . . SPLAT! Into the mud they would go. If they got tired and couldn't make it . . . SPLAT! Right down into the mud they would go.

"Wisp will be the leader for the first obstacle," said Zeena. "He will direct the rest of you."

"Oh, man," Wisp said. "That's a lot of pressure!"

"You can do it," said Norm. He gave Wisp a big thumbs-up.

"Blindfolds on, Creature Campers," said Grumplestick. "And no peeking. Peeking will get you disqualified."

"That doesn't sound so bad," Oliver said.

"And if you are disqualified," continued Grumplestick, "you'll have to wash all of the camp's dirty dishes for the rest of the summer."

"Gross!" said Oliver. He put his blindfold

on and tied it tight. "I can't see a thing!"

"That's the idea," said Zeena.

"How many fingers am I holding up?" asked Grumplestick.

"How am I supposed to know?" replied Oliver. "I can't even see my own hand, let alone yours!"

"Good," said Grumplestick. "That was a test."

Norm and Hazel tied their blindfolds on as well.

"Can you guys hear me?" Wisp asked.

"Loud and clear," Norm said.

"Sure can!" Hazel said.

"Like you're standing right in front of me," Oliver said.

"That's because I am," Wisp said.

"Okay, campers," Grumplestick said.

"Get ready. On your mark, get set . . . go!"

When he said "go," Zeena started the stopwatch with a click.

"Norm, you go first," Wisp said. "Reach up and grab the first bar. It's right over your head."

Norm reached up but felt nothing.

"Too high," said Wisp. "You reached right past the bar. Lower . . . lower . . . still lower. Got it!"

Norm wrapped his fingers tightly around the bar and waited for Wisp to direct him.

"Reach forward with your other arm," Wisp said. "Just a bit more . . . "

Norm stretched out his right arm and felt for the bar. Once he had hold of it, he let go with his left and swung his body forward. Wisp helped him find the next bar, and just like that, Norm was across.

"I thought there were more than three bars," Norm said, still blindfolded and standing on the other side of the mud pit.

"There are," said Wisp. "You just skipped them."

Hazel was next. She scrambled up and grabbed the first bar.

Wisp stood by the side of the mud pit and said, "Reach forward and grab the—"

"Grab the first bar?" Hazel said. "Got it. Got the first bar. Then what do I do? Where's

the next bar? Where's the next bar, Wisp? Am I close? Am I hot? Am I cold? Am I getting warmer?"

"Just swing forward a little and—"

"And what? Swing forward and what, Wisp? What should I swing forward and do?"

"I'm trying to tell you!" Wisp said. "Swing forward and find the next bar. You're just about—"

"I'm stuck!" said Hazel. "Something got me! What got me? Save me!"

"Nothing got you," Wisp said. "Your antlers are just stuck between the bars! Stop moving!"

Hazel's feet kicked the air and one hand waved around, feeling for the next bar.

Wisp squeezed his eyes shut, took a

deep breath, and fluttered his wings as fast as he could. Little by little, he lifted off the ground until he was right in front of Hazel, hovering above the mud.

"Take a deep breath," he said.

Hazel took a deep breath.

"Grab this bar." Wisp directed her hand to the bar. "Now turn your head sideways."

Hazel did what Wisp said. Her antlers came unstuck. Wisp guided her the rest of the way across.

"Are we there yet?" she asked, swinging to the next bar and the next and the next. "Are we there yet? Are we there yet? Are we there yet? Are we—YES!" Hazel dropped down off the monkey bars and felt her way over to Norm.

Oliver was next. He grabbed the first bar and hung over the mud.

"Reach up and out and grab the next bar," Wisp said.

"I can't hold myself up!" Oliver said. He held on as tight as he could, but his fingers were slipping. Just as Oliver was about to fall into the mud, Wisp flew underneath him. He pushed up with all his might.

It was almost, but not quite, enough to keep Oliver from falling off.

Just as his fingers slipped off the bar, a small, orange life preserver attached to a rope descended from above, dangling *just* within Oliver's reach. Wisp didn't see it because he was underneath Oliver, trying to hold him up. Zeena and Grumplestick didn't see it because they were looking at the stopwatch.

Oliver grabbed the life preserver and held on.

MEANWHILE . . .

From the basket of a newly patched hot air balloon, a long rope dangled all the way down to the monkey bars. In the balloon's basket, Barnaby Snoop held on to one end of the rope and braced himself as Oliver put all of his weight on the life preserver at the other end.

"Just a little boost," Barnaby huffed. "A little help goes a long way."

"Just. A. Bit. More," Wisp gasped as Oliver let go of the life preserver and moved to the next bar, and then the next. The life preserver continued to hover above

Oliver while Barnaby Snoop watched anxiously.

Finally, they reached the far side of the mud pit. The life preserver slipped back up into the clouds before anyone could see it.

Oliver and Wisp collapsed to the ground, exhausted.

"Great teamwork!" Zeena said. She looked up from the stopwatch. "The tire crawl is next. Oliver, you're the new leader."

"I don't think I want to be the leader," Oliver said.

"You'll be a fine leader," said Zeena. "Just be confident."

"Yeah," said Norm, "just like when you led us north by knowing how moss grew on trees during our map and compass test. That was great!"

Oliver took a deep breath. "Okay. Confident."

As Wisp put on his blindfold, Oliver pulled his off. Then Oliver called out, "Okay, everyone—hold on to each other and follow my voice!"

The tire crawl was a tunnel made of twelve tires of all different sizes. The bottom half of each tire was buried in the dirt, forming an upside-down U. The campers were going to have to crawl through the tunnel, sometimes wiggling on their bellies in order to get through the smaller tires.

"I have a plan," Oliver said. "It'll probably fail, but—"

Norm patted around in front of himself until he found Oliver's shoulder, and then he patted it. "It'll work. I believe in you."

Oliver smiled up at Norm. Then he knelt down and unlaced his shoes. He tied one shoelace from Wisp's waist to Norm's left wrist.

"We'll crawl single file," Oliver said. "Wisp, I'll guide you. Norm, you follow Wisp."

Then he tied the other shoelace from Norm's ankle to Hazel's antlers.

"Hazel, you follow Norm," he said. "Ready?"

"Ready!" said Wisp.

"Lead the way!" said Norm.

"Let's do this!" said Hazel.

"Is that allowed?" Grumplestick asked Zeena, lifting his whistle to his lips.

"I don't see why not," she replied. "That's good problem-solving!"

"I guess you're right," Grumplestick grumbled as he let his whistle drop.

Oliver led them through the first

several tires. Some they went through on their hands and knees. Others they slithered under like snakes. Everything was fine until they got to the last tire.

It was very low. Very, *very* low.

Oliver pulled himself through on his belly, digging his elbows into the dirt. Wisp followed after him with no trouble.

"Maybe being small isn't so bad after all," Wisp said.

But when Norm tried to go through . . . "Guys?" he said. "I think I'm stuck." He tried to pull himself forward, but he couldn't budge. He tried to wiggle backward, but he couldn't budge. He was definitely stuck halfway through the tire.

"This could really hurt your time," Zeena called out.

MEANWHILE...

Barnaby Snoop groaned. They had been doing so well!

"Think, Barnaby, think!" he said to himself.

Barnaby's eyes fell on the anchor he used to hold his hot air balloon in place.

"Aha!" he said. "Barnaby, you are one brilliant fellow!"

He grabbed the anchor and the rope and leaned over the edge, waiting for just the right moment.

"Wisp, grab Norm's wrist," Oliver said. "When I say go, you pull as hard as you can.

Hazel, you push. And Norm?"

"Yes?"

"Suck in your stomach as far as you can."

"And stop eating so much berry casserole," Hazel mumbled.

"I heard that!" Norm said.

"Go!" Oliver shouted.

Norm sucked in his stomach. Oliver and Wisp pulled. Hazel pushed. But Norm did not budge an inch.

Grumplestick shook his head and turned to look toward the invisible wall.

"See that?" he asked.

"No," said Zeena. "It's still invisible. There's nothing to see."

"Exactly," said Grumplestick. "You won't see their names on the wall."

While Grumplestick and Zeena were talking, an anchor slipped down from above and caught the top edge of the tire that Norm was trapped in. Oliver did not see it because he was tugging so hard that his eyes were squeezed shut. Grumplestick and Zeena did not see it because they were looking at an invisible wall.

But Barnaby Snoop watched it hook on the tire and got ready to pull as hard as he could.

"Norm?" Hazel said.

"Yes?"

"I apologize in advance," said Hazel.

"For wha—YEOW!"

Hazel lowered her pointy antlers and charged forward. The antlers poked Norm right on his rump at the exact same moment that Barnaby yanked up on the rope and anchor, stretching the tire as wide as it would go. Norm yelped and lunged forward, popping out of the tire.

As soon as Norm was through, Barnaby yanked the anchor back up into the clouds.

When Grumplestick and Zeena turned back around, Norm was through the tire, rubbing his sore behind. Hazel had Bigfoot fur on her antlers and was scrambling through the tire after Norm.

"Good job, Creature Campers," said Zeena. "And now it's time for . . ."

"The wall!" Grumplestick said.

The campers pulled off their blindfolds and looked ahead. At first there was nothing there, and then the wall winked into view. It loomed above the campers, casting a very dark shadow over them.

Norm, Oliver, Wisp, and Hazel all gulped.

"At least we can see it now," Norm said.

"New batteries," said Zeena, holding up the controller.

Wisp groaned. "I almost wish I *couldn't* see it."

"*You* won't, Wisp," Grumplestick said. "Norm is the leader this time."

"Yes!" Norm said. "Finally!"

"Drat," said Hazel.

"I was hoping I could be the leader. When do I get a turn being the leader? Can I be the leader next?"

Norm's grin faded. Hazel *really* wanted to be the leader. Wisp had a turn, Oliver had a turn, and now, if Norm was the leader for the last obstacle, Hazel wouldn't get a turn. Unless . . .

"Hazel can be the leader," Norm said. "She'll do as good a job as any of us."

"Really?" asked Hazel. "I can be the leader? You'll let me be the leader? I really get to be—"

"Yes, Hazel," said Zeena. "You are the leader."

"Yay!" said Hazel.

"Lead the way," said Norm. "Next stop: the other side of that wall!"

The wall looked a lot bigger as they got closer—and it had already looked pretty big from far away.

The Creature Campers stood at the foot of the wall and looked up toward the sky. A lone wind sock flapped in the breeze on the platform at the top.

"All you have to do is climb up this side and down the other side," said Grumplestick. "It's as easy as that."

"But it's so high!" Wisp said.

"And steep," Hazel said.

"And scary," Oliver said.

"Well of course it is," said Grumplestick. "It's a challenge! Okay, blindfolds on!"

"I changed my mind," said Hazel. "I don't want to be the leader. I want Norm to be the leader."

"You do?" Norm asked.

"Are you sure?" asked Zeena.

Hazel looked up at the wall, towering over her. "I'm sure I'm sure."

"Okay," said Zeena. "Norm, you are now the leader."

Norm pulled off his blindfold, took a

deep breath, and studied the wall. It was very, very tall, and there was one rope dangling from the top.

"I have a plan," Norm said.

"Does your plan involve turning around and going back to our cabin?" Oliver asked.

"Or going around the wall?" Wisp asked.

"Or through it?" Hazel asked while putting her blindfold back on.

"That doesn't even make sense, Hazel," Norm said. "But no, to all of those. We're going over that wall and getting our names on it."

Grumplestick yawned loudly. "Looks like ol' Grumplestick here is going to remain the champion."

Zeena checked her stopwatch. "Unless,

of course, you can get your entire team over that wall in three minutes."

Norm wrapped his arms around his friends and pulled them close.

"Everybody listen," he said. "We have one chance to do this. If we do it right, we

can get up and over this wall in three minutes and beat Grumplestick's time."

"What's the plan?" Wisp asked.

"Ooh, I know," said Hazel. "Does it involve broccoli, two sticks, and a jar of marbles?"

"Wait, what?" asked Norm.

"Hazel," said Oliver, "sometimes you worry me."

"Here's how we get to the top," Norm said as he leaned in and whispered to his friends.

MEANWHILE...

A shadow swooped overhead.

"What is *that*?" Barnaby asked as the shadow landed on top of the wall.

Barnaby held his telescope to his eye. "It can't be!" he said. "That's a rare red-billed flying porcupinesnake. And she's protecting her eggs! If those Creature Campers get anywhere near her, she'll..."

Barnaby put down his telescope. "Well, old fellow," he said, "it's time for action."

Ever so slowly, Barnaby's hot air balloon descended toward the top of the wall.

"Is everyone ready?" Norm asked.

"Ready," said Wisp.

"Aye, aye, captain!" said Hazel.

"No?" said Oliver. "But . . . okay."

Norm stepped forward. "Let's do this," he said.

Zeena started her stopwatch. "Two minutes and fifty-nine seconds," she called. "Good luck, Creature Campers!"

Wisp was the first to climb the rope. He took a very deep breath, held the rope tight, and fluttered his little wings as fast as he could.

"Am I there yet?" he asked.

"Let's just say you have a lot more to go," Norm said.

Wisp fluttered his wings harder. He

took a deeper breath. He pushed higher.

"Am I close?" Wisp called down.

"Keep going, Wisp," Norm said. "You're doing great!"

"You've got this, Wisp!" Oliver cheered.

"You can do it!" Hazel called up.

Wisp was getting tired. He was running out of breath. He was fluttering his wings as fast and as hard as he could.

"Don't . . . give . . . up," he said through gritted teeth.

And then, suddenly, he was at the top of the rope. He'd done it! He'd flown higher than he ever had before.

"Stop right there!" Norm hollered up.

Wisp climbed onto the platform and stopped.

"It's very windy up here!" he called down. He was glad he was blindfolded. He'd never been this high up, not even with wings. He was not like the other fairies. His one smaller wing kept him very close to the ground.

"It's so windy that it sounds like something is hissing!" Wisp called down.

Something was, indeed, hissing. And it was not the wind.

MEANWHILE...

Barnaby's balloon floated just above the far side of the wall, out of sight of the Creature Campers but close enough that he could leap out to help Wisp before the rare red-billed flying porcupinesnake swallowed the fairy whole.

The long, spiky, feathered snake reared up, wings back, red-billed mouth open wide, and struck.

Barnaby grabbed Wisp and pulled him out of the way just in time. The porcupinesnake's teeth crunched into the space where Wisp had just been, grabbing nothing but air.

"Wow!" Wisp called down. "The wind is blowing me all over the place!"

Barnaby quickly ducked under the porcupinesnake. He snatched the wind sock and waved it back and forth like a matador taunting a charging bull.

The porcupinesnake hissed and coiled for another strike.

Back on the ground, Norm was getting ready to guide the next Creature Camper up the wall.

"Hold on to the railing!" Norm called up to Wisp. "And when I say NOW! you catch Hazel."

Wisp's voice drifted down. "Ready!"

"Oh, man," Oliver said. "It sounds like he's a mile above us.

Are you sure about this, Norm?"

"Mostly?" Norm said.

"Mostly?" said Oliver. "You know, sometimes it's okay to fib a little. Like, tell me you're 100 percent sure about this."

"I am 97 percent sure about this," Norm said.

"That's not a hundred!"

"Well, I don't feel comfortable fibbing!" said Norm.

"Is it my turn yet?" Hazel asked.

"Sure is," said Norm.

"Really sure," mumbled Oliver, "or like 97 percent sure?"

Norm led Hazel a few feet back from the base of the wall.

"When I say go, you run as fast as you can. Don't stop until Wisp stops you."

He went back and knelt at the base of the obstacle. He cupped his hands together.

"Three, two, one . . . go!" Norm shouted.

Hazel sprinted forward as fast as her little legs would carry her. As soon as she reached Norm, he heaved her up into the air, like a springboard. Hazel's still-running feet hit the wall about halfway up, and her speed carried her to the top.

"Wheeeeeee!"

"Now, Wisp!" Norm yelled.

Wisp reached out, feeling for Hazel, and his hands came within inches of grabbing the porcupinesnake's tail.

"Over here!" Barnaby called, doing his best Hazel impersonation.

"Hazel?" Wisp said, turning away from the porcupinesnake just in time.

Hazel ran right into Wisp and the two of them fell back onto the platform, landing right between Barnaby and the porcupinesnake.

"You sound different," Wisp said.

"I didn't say anything," Hazel said.

Wisp shrugged. "Must have been the howling wind."

"Fifty-seven seconds!" Zeena told the

campers, her eyes on the stopwatch. Grumplestick was beginning to look a little nervous. Nobody had ever beaten his time. He took the stopwatch from Zeena, shaking it back and forth.

"Are you sure this thing is right?" he asked.

"I calibrated it myself," said Zeena. She took the stopwatch back.

"Our turn," Norm said. He clapped Oliver on the shoulder. "I know you're nervous about this, and so am I, but trust me. We can do this."

"O-o-okay," said Oliver. "I-I trust you."

Norm grabbed the rope and tied it around Oliver's waist.

"As soon as I'm up, I'll pull you to the top," said Norm.

Oliver gave him a shaky thumbs-up.

"Forty-three seconds," said Zeena.

"Here I go," said Norm. He reached up and grasped the rope.

As Norm climbed, the rare red-billed flying porcupinesnake fluffed its wings and snapped its fanged mouth at Barnaby.

But Barnaby Snoop, creature collector and carnival owner, happened to be an expert in the study of rare flying species and knew a thing or two about rare red-billed flying porcupinesnakes. Just as it was about to strike, he whistled as loud as he could.

The porcupinesnake hissed and coiled into a ball, ducking its head under its body to avoid the high-pitched sound.

In the blink of an eye, Barnaby leapt

past Hazel and Wisp and brought the wind sock down on the porcupinesnake's head, covering its eyes and red-billed mouth. It thrashed right. It thrashed left. It thrashed up and down, and Barnaby hung on for dear life. He hooked one toe on the edge of the balloon basket and pulled himself and the porcupinesnake into it.

The second they landed in the small basket, Barnaby cut the weighted sandbags that had held the balloon above the wall, and the hot air balloon drifted up and into the cover of the clouds.

The porcupinesnake shook the wind sock off its head and hissed at Barnaby.

Barnaby snatched up his little stool and held it between them as the wind sock drifted down and landed on top of the wall.

With his long legs and long reach, Norm was at the top in ten pulls.

"Norm?" Oliver called from below.

"Hold on tight!" Norm said.

Before Oliver knew it, he was yanked off his feet and up, up, up into the air. He landed on top of the platform with Wisp, Hazel, and Norm.

"Now I know what a yo-yo feels like," said Oliver.

"Twenty-three seconds!" Zeena called out.

Grumplestick was sweating.

Norm snatched up the wind sock that had landed on top of the platform and handed it to Hazel. Then he quickly pulled the laces back out of Oliver's shoes.

"Oliver, Wisp, when it's time, hang your laces over the rope and hold on with both hands. Hazel, do the same with your wind sock. Once I tell you to slide, you hold on as tight as you can and step off the platform."

"Off!?" Oliver said.

"Off of the platform!?" cried Wisp.

"Are you CRAZY!?" asked Hazel.

"I got you to the top, didn't I?" asked Norm.

"Yes," they grumbled.

"Fifteen seconds!" Zeena said.

Grumplestick chewed on his hat.

"Then trust me," said Norm. "I'll see you at the bottom."

He grasped the rope and bounded

down the back of the wall. He made it in seven leaps.

"Ten seconds!"

"Slide!" Norm said. He held the rope out at a slight angle, pulling it as tight as he could.

Wisp went first.

"Aaaaaahhhh!" He slid down the rope and landed next to Norm.

"Eight seconds!" said Zeena.

Hazel went next.

"Geronimoooooooo!"

She slid down the rope and landed next to Wisp and Norm.

"Seven seconds!" called Zeena.

Oliver stood, shaking, at the edge of the platform. The wind rustled his hair. His toes dangled over the edge.

"Oliver!" Norm shouted. "You have to go!"

"I'm scared!" Oliver shouted back.

"I will 100 percent catch you!" Norm said.

"Three seconds!" said Zeena.

Grumplestick held his breath.

Oliver tightened his grip on his shoelace and stepped off the platform.

"AAAAAAaaaaaaahhhhhhhhhh!" he

screamed, sliding down the rope and landing in Norm's arms.

Zeena clicked the button on her stopwatch.

Grumplestick exhaled.

Wisp, Hazel, and Oliver took off their blindfolds.

"I don't feel so good," said Oliver.

He looked a little green.

"Well?" said Norm. "Did we do it?"

"Did they beat my time?" asked Grumplestick. "They didn't beat my time. They couldn't have beaten my time!"

Zeena held up the stopwatch so everyone could see it.

They had 0.2 seconds to spare.

"We did it!" Norm said.

"Yay for us! Wall of fame, here we come!" said Oliver.

Wisp and Hazel high-fived.

Grumplestick crossed his arms. "Well I'll be a pickled gnome," he said. "You didn't just beat the course, you also beat my time. Looks like your names will be going up on the wall—"

"Of DOOM!" shouted Norm, Oliver,

Wisp, and Hazel, all at the same time.

"No doom," sighed Grumplestick. "You've earned it, Creature Campers. That was great teamwork."

Zeena, however, was watching the sky.

"Um, Furrow?" she said. "Do you happen to know anything about a hot air balloon being a part of the course?"

"What? No," said Grumplestick. "Camp Moonlight doesn't have a hot air balloon."

Zeena pointed one long, slender finger toward the sky. The clouds had cleared, revealing a swaying, spinning, rocking hot air balloon.

"Then what is that?" she asked.

Barnaby Snoop ran in circles around the little basket, trying to avoid the hissing porcupinesnake.

The porcupinesnake snapped its mouth shut and sucked air in, swelling up until it nearly filled the basket.

Then its spiky quills shot out like

needles and popped the hot air balloon.

"Look," said Oliver. "It's Mister Mustache! And he's in trouble!"

"Who's Mister Mustache, and how do you know him?" Grumplestick asked.

"He's the nice man we met during our map and compass challenge," said Wisp.

"And we saw him in Shadow Lake when we were doing our canoeing skills test, too," said Norm.

"Well, what on earth is he doing here?" Grumplestick asked.

"By the looks of things," said Zeena, "I would say he's crashing."

As the air rushed out of the punctured hot air balloon, the rare red-billed flying porcupinesnake launched itself into the air and glided back to the wall.

Meanwhile, the ground was getting closer, and closer, and CLOSER to Barnaby Snoop.

"We have to help him!" said Norm.

"Don't worry, Mister Mustache!" he hollered up. "We're going to save you! Just throw us a rope!"

Barnaby Snoop fumbled around the basket floor for a coil of rope. Grabbing it with shaking hands, he tossed one end over the edge of the balloon basket.

"Here's the plan," Norm said.

Zeena and Grumplestick quickly moved the monkey bars away from above the ooey, gooey mud pit.

Norm handed Hazel and Oliver the rope Barnaby had dropped down. "When I say go, we all need to run as fast as we can toward the mud pit."

Hazel and Oliver held the rope tight and nodded.

"Wisp," said Norm. "Think you have a little energy left in those wings?"

Wisp fluttered his wings. "Ready for liftoff," he said.

Norm lifted Wisp up over his head, Wisp pinned his arms to his sides and stuck out his wings. Norm pulled his arm back and threw Wisp through the air like a paper airplane.

"Woohoo!" Wisp called, soaring straight toward the top of the balloon.

As soon as he was above the collapsed

balloon, he reached down and grabbed it, flapping his wings as fast as he could and pulling up with all of his little strength.

"Go, go, go!" Norm shouted as he grabbed the rope.

Oliver, Hazel, and Norm shot off toward the mud pit. With the three of them pulling the balloon and Wisp giving it just a little bit of a lift, the basket glided to a landing in the middle of the mud pit.

Barnaby Snoop staggered out of the hot air balloon basket and nearly collapsed. But before he had a chance to fall, Norm reached out to help him.

"Don't worry, Mister Mustache," Norm said. "You're safe with us."

Perhaps it was something in his eye, or perhaps he was allergic to mud, or perhaps . . . perhaps Barnaby Snoop actually felt overwhelmed by the fact that this Bigfoot and all of these Creature Campers had gone out of their way to save him.

Barnaby Snoop knew that from that

day forward, he was going to help creatures, not cage them.

He wiped the tear from his eye and smiled at Oliver, Norm, Hazel, and Wisp.

"Thank you," he said.

The next day, Norm took an early walk to look at the wall. Written right above Furrow Grumplestick's name were four more names.

Norm couldn't wait for visiting day, when Ma and Pa would come to see him at camp. He was going to take them to see the

wall. But before that, he was going to make sure they met his best friends.

However, visiting day was still a couple days away, and today they had a new event scheduled.

Zeena gathered the campers together to introduce the camp's newest staff member.

"Creature Campers, I'd like you to meet Camp Moonlight's newest animal expert, Mister Barnaby Snoop."

Much to everyone's surprise, the man who was standing before them was none other than Mister Mustache.

"Mister Mustache!" they said.

"It's Mister Snoop," he corrected. "And today we are going to observe the hatching of a rare red-billed flying porcupinesnake egg. The nest is right at the top of the wall . . . of DOOM!"

Everyone burst out laughing. Even Grumplestick couldn't help but chuckle.

"Camp Moonlight," Norm said happily. "It's not just fun . . . "

"It's *FUNusual!*" all the best friends shouted together.

ALL ABOUT... OBSTACLE COURSES!

Camp Moonlight's obstacle course has it all: climbing, running, mud, and a little bit of doom! (That is, if you believe Grumplestick.) In real life, obstacle courses have been popular for thousands of years. The one the Creature Campers completed isn't so different from the very first courses that were part of the ancient Olympic Games in Greece.

Early obstacle courses included events

like the discus throw, footraces, distance jumping, and wrestling. They were designed to test speed, strength, and endurance, which means how long a person can handle a physical challenge.

Today's obstacle courses take place all over the world and attract people of all ages and skill levels. Like the one at Camp Moonlight, they're usually timed, and sometimes they even involve messy mud pits. (But no other course has a rare red-billed flying porcupinesnake!)